# A Funny First Day

Catherine Mangieri

# NEIGHBORHOOD READERS

Rosen Classroom Books & Materials™

New York

I am going to school today.
It is the first day of school.

The cat eats my breakfast.
Oh no!

The dog eats my socks.
Oh no!

A bird takes my toothbrush.
Oh no!
Come back!

A squirrel takes my lunch.
Oh no!

A raccoon takes my book.
Oh no!
Come back!

7

A skunk takes my hat.
Oh no!

Dad takes my umbrella.
Oh no!
I am going to get wet!

The bus is here.
Oh no!
I am late!

I lose my shoe.
Oh no!
Where is my shoe?

What a funny first day!